SPORTS GREAT DAVID ROBINSON

Revised Edition

—Sports Great Books—

BASEBALL

Sports Great Jim Abbott
0-89490-395-0/ Savage

Sports Great Barry Bonds
0-89490-595-3/ Sullivan

Sports Great Bobby Bonilla
0-89490-417-5/ Knapp

Sports Great Orel Hershiser
0-89490-389-6/ Knapp

Sports Great Bo Jackson
0-89490-281-4/ Knapp

Sports Great Greg Maddux
0-89490-873-1/ Thornley

Sports Great Kirby Puckett
0-89490-392-6/ Aaseng

Sports Great Cal Ripken, Jr.
0-89490-387-X/ Macnow

Sports Great Nolan Ryan
0-89490-394-2/ Lace

Sports Great Darryl Strawberry
0-89490-291-1/ Torres & Sullivan

BASKETBALL

Sports Great Charles Barkley
(Revised)
0-7660-1004-X/ Macnow

Sports Great Larry Bird
0-89490-368-3/ Kavanagh

Sports Great Muggsy Bogues
0-89490-876-6/ Rekela

Sports Great Patrick Ewing
0-89490-369-1/ Kavanagh

Sports Great Anfernee Hardaway
0-89490-758-1/ Rekela

Sports Great Magic Johnson
Revised and Expanded
0-89490-348-9/ Haskins

Sports Great Michael Jordan
Revised Edition
0-89490-978-9/ Aaseng

Sports Great Jason Kidd
0-7660-1001-5/ Torres

Sports Great Karl Malone
0-89490-599-6/ Savage

Sports Great Reggie Miller
0-89490-874-X/ Thornley

Sports Great Alonzo Mourning
0-89490-875-8/ Fortunato

Sports Great Hakeem Olajuwon
0-89490-372-1/ Knapp

Sports Great Shaquille O'Neal
0-89490-594-5/ Sullivan

Sports Great Scottie Pippen
0-89490-755-7/ Bjarkman

Sports Great David Robinson
(Revised)
0-7660-1077-5/ Aaseng

Sports Great Dennis Rodman
0-89490-759-X/ Thornley

Sports Great John Stockton
0-89490-598-8/ Aaseng

Sports Great Isiah Thomas
0-89490-374-8/ Knapp

Sports Great Dominique Wilkins
0-89490-754-9/ Bjarkman

FOOTBALL

Sports Great Troy Aikman
0-89490-593-7/ Macnow

Sports Great Jerome Bettis
0-89490-872-3/Majewski

Sports Great John Elway
0-89490-282-2/ Fox

Sports Great Brett Favre
0-7660-1000-7/ Savage

Sports Great Jim Kelly
0-89490-670-4/ Harrington

Sports Great Joe Montana
0-89490-371-3/ Kavanagh

Sports Great Jerry Rice
0-89490-419-1/ Dickey

Sports Great Barry Sanders
0-89490-418-3/ Knapp

Sports Great Emmitt Smith
0-7660-1002-3/ Grabowski

Sports Great Herschel Walker
0-89490-207-5/ Benagh

HOCKEY

Sports Great Wayne Gretzky
0-89490-757-3/ Rappoport

Sports Great Mario Lemieux
0-89490-596-1/ Knapp

Sports Great Eric Lindros
0-89490-871-5/ Rappoport

TENNIS

Sports Great Steffi Graf
0-89490-597-X/ Knapp

Sports Great Pete Sampras
0-89490-756-5/ Sherrow

SPORTS GREAT
DAVID
ROBINSON

Revised Edition

Nathan Aaseng

—Sports Great Books—

Enslow Publishers, Inc.

44 Fadem Road	PO Box 38
Box 699	Aldershot
Springfield, NJ 07081	Hants GU12 6BP
USA	UK

Library of Congress Cataloging-in-Publication Data

Aaseng, Nathan.
    Sports great David Robinson / Nathan Aaseng. — Rev. ed.
      p. cm. — (Sports great books)
    Includes bibliographical references (p.) and index.
    Summary: Describes the personal life and basketball career of the defensive star for
the San Antonio Spurs, who also achieved success at the Naval Academy and on the
1992 and 1996 Olympic "Dream Teams."
     ISBN 0-7660-1077-5
     1. Robinson, David, 1965– —Juvenile literature. 2. Basketball players—United
States—Biography—Juvenile literature. 3. San Antonio Spurs (Basketball team)—
Juvenile literature. [1. Robinson, David, 1965– . 2. Basketball players.
3. Afro-Americans—Biography.] I. Title. II. Series.
GV884.R615A615 1998
796.323'092—dc21
[B]   97-14982
                                                 CIP
                                                   AC

Printed in the United States of America

10 9 8 7 6 5 4 3 2 1

Illustration Credits: © D. Clarke Evans, p. 31; © Norm Purdue, pp. 12, 38, 46, 53,
56; © Norm Purdue, 1996, pp. 8, 10, 36, 40, 44, 49, 59; University of Pittsburgh,
p. 23; U.S. Department of Defense, D.E. Erickson, p. 17; U.S. Navy, pp. 20, 29.

Cover Illustration: © Norm Purdue, 1996.

Contents

Chapter 1

The crowd noise nearly blew off the roof of the Alamodome in San Antonio, Texas, as the public address announcer called the name of David Robinson. The Spurs' graceful, seven-foot one-inch center strode with his usual, ramrod straight posture to center court.

This was all new to Robinson. Never before had his team advanced to the Western Conference finals. A win in this series against the Houston Rockets would send the Spurs into the 1995 National Basketball Association (NBA) Finals. Unfortunately, the Spurs had begun the best-of-seven series with a heartbreaking loss. In order to send the stomping, howling home fans into a frenzy, the team had arranged to present its star player with a trophy before the game. Robinson would receive the NBA's 1994–95 Most Valuable Player (MVP) award that he had earned with his brilliant all-around play.

Robinson soaked up the thunderous applause. This was a startling honor for someone who had hardly played the game as a boy. It was a tremendous accomplishment for a man who

Robinson demonstrates a new offensive weapon he has added to his arsenal—a hook shot.

had entered the league with a dunk shot as his only scoring weapon.

Inspired by the event, Robinson went out and played an exceptional game. He connected on 10 of 18 shots from the field and added 12 free throws for 32 points. He crashed the boards to collect 12 rebounds. When his team needed him the most—in the crucial fourth quarter—Robinson played his best. He scored 14 of his points in the final period. All of this came against Hakeem Olajuwon, one of the best centers ever to play in the NBA.

Yet the evening that had started so well ended up a disaster. In these playoffs, Olajuwon had raised his game to a new level. He frustrated Robinson with a bewildering assortment of spins, fakes, and off-balance shots. In the end Olajuwon walked off the court with 41 points as the Rockets defeated the Spurs, 106-96.

The evening was typical of David Robinson's career in pro basketball. Few men have bounced around between glorious highs and rock-bottom lows the way Robinson has.

In many ways Robinson is a coach's dream. Despite his height, he can dribble as well as a small guard. He is so coordinated he can walk across a gymnasium on his hands. With his trim body (his waist is only thirty-three inches around) and lean legs, he can sprint down the court faster than any seven-footer who ever played the game. Yet his upper body ripples with muscle. He has built himself up to a powerful 245 pounds so that he can hold his own in rugged turf wars for position against enormous opponents such as Shaquille O'Neal.

Robinson's size, speed, and coordination allow him to do things other big men can't. Other centers can soar high to block a shot or snatch the ball out of the air or fire a pass to a guard in the open court. Yet Robinson can also catch up to the

Robinson's speed allows him to break free from defenders in the lane so that he can catch passes and score.

action, take the pass, and finish the fast break with a monster dunk—all before the defense can get set!

Veteran NBA coach Cotton Fitzsimmons called Robinson "the greatest impact player the league has seen since Kareem Abdul-Jabbar." Others say that Robinson reminds them of Bill Russell—the most intimidating defender who ever played basketball. Except, they say, Robinson is taller, faster, and more athletic.

Robinson is also one of the most intelligent athletes in NBA history. He accepts coaching well. He is polite and respectful—almost to a fault. To top it all off, many NBA observers consider Robinson the best role model for kids of all the basketball players in the league.

Then again, this dream player has sometimes been a coach's nightmare. Few pro athletes have made it as far as Robinson has with so little interest in their sport. Robinson played just one year of basketball before entering college, and he did that reluctantly. He knew so little about the game that his coach at the United States Naval Academy felt as though he were working with a high school freshman.

Although he rapidly became the best player in the country, Robinson insisted that basketball was just something he did for fun. He shook his head in disbelief at teammates who would actually work on their game after practice had ended. He had other interests that were at least as important as basketball. Robinson enjoyed playing the piano or solving an advanced mathematical problem.

For sports fanatics who thought athletes should eat, sleep, and breath their sport, Robinson's approach to the game was like hearing fingernails scratch a chalkboard. One coach after another felt he was beating his head against a wall trying to get Robinson to take the sport more seriously.

Sometimes Robinson's mind wandered even when he was

Robinson, in a rare moment, takes a breather and studies the action from the bench.

trying to pay attention. In his early years in the league, he often drifted into his own world even in the middle of a game. One of his pro coaches sighed, "I don't know where David goes when he loses his concentration."

In many ways David Robinson has been a fish out of water among NBA stars. Experts questioned whether a man with so many talents and outside interests could ever devote himself to the game enough to become the best. Many observers stated that Robinson was too much of a gentleman to display the toughness and fierce competitive fire that a champion needs.

He has struggled to find himself in the fast-paced world of pro sports. As his teammate Sean Elliot observed, "This league changes everyone who comes into it. David was no different." In a career that has regularly plunged like a roller coaster through incredible highs and lows, Robinson has had to ask himself some tough questions.

In answering those questions, Robinson has found out what is important to him in life. After years of indifference, he has dedicated himself to living up to his potential as one of the best big men ever to play basketball. More importantly, he knows that he wants to do it the right way. Through triumph and defeat, Robinson stands apart from many of his cocky, trash-talking, self-promoting peers. He has learned to keep his balance on the slippery path of fame.

Chapter 2

Ambrose Robinson knew what it was to perform under pressure. As a high school student in Little Rock, Arkansas, Robinson had scored well on a college entrance exam. It should have been a proud moment for him. However, in a time of racial unrest, his score drew only anger and suspicion. Test officials refused to believe that Robinson, who was black, could score so much higher than most of the white students. They accused him of cheating.

Robinson was forced to retake the exam under the hostile glare of test officials. Any slipup on his part would be considered proof that he had cheated. Ambrose Robinson met the challenge. He scored even higher the second time than he had the first! His success on the test opened the way to a distinguished career as a submarine sonar radar technician in the United States Navy.

Ambrose and his wife Freda were stationed in Key West, Florida, when their second child David Maurice Robinson was born on August 6, 1965. David inherited a great deal of his father's brilliance, and then some.

In Virginia Beach, Virginia, where the Robinsons moved shortly after David's birth, David showed an amazing ability to learn. He was placed in a special program for gifted children as soon as he entered first grade. One of his favorite games as a small child was to add up his mother's grocery bill in his head before the cart was unloaded at the checkout line.

Ambrose Robinson was a demanding teacher. He insisted that his young son read through the entire dictionary to improve his vocabulary. When David came home with an A, two Bs, and a C on his report card in junior high, his dad grounded him for six weeks.

Ambrose, however, was not the competitive type. When principals suggested that David be moved up a grade in school, Ambrose said no. Rather than pushing David to excel at any one thing, he kept encouraging him to try new things.

Ambrose taught him a few basic notes on the piano. Without a formal lesson, David learned to play classical music by ear.

Ambrose taught him basic electronics. When the elder Robinson was shipped out to sea before putting together a widescreen TV he had bought, twelve-year-old David installed it on his own. The boy even figured out how to solder the connections without having ever soldered before. At the age of fourteen, David enrolled in an advanced computer course. Although he did not follow sports closely, and was not very good at them, he went out for a half dozen sports as a youth.

David not only developed the same wide-ranging curiosity as his dad, he also picked up his father's laid-back attitude and wandering attention span. Freda Robinson was not about to let her son coast along, dabbling in whatever caught his fancy. She encouraged him to set goals and accomplish something with his talents.

Their parents' busy work schedules forced the Robinson children to accept a great deal of responsibility. Ambrose Robinson was often sent out to sea aboard submarines. He could be away from home for as long as six months at a time. Freda worked full-time as a nurse. That often left David, his older sister Kim, and younger brother Chuck to cook their own meals, do the housework, and get their homework done without being nagged.

Despite the absences and the extra work, the Robinson household was exceptionally calm and stress-free. "I had responsibility, but I had freedom too," Robinson says. "So I never had a desire to break loose." The family was very close, and the only hero David ever had was his dad. It was his dream to follow him into the Navy, and go on to a career in science.

As a boy, David Robinson considered sports to be nothing more than one of life's many curiosities. In some ways he did not fit in with other boys. He took what people said so literally that most jokes went over his head. Sports were not as easy for him as most things that he attempted, and so he did not develop much confidence in his skill. He tried out for basketball during his freshman year of high school and found himself sitting on the bench. When he thought his coach was going to cut him from the team, David quit. He also found it difficult to focus on the many routine drills that are a part of all sports learning. Robinson dropped out of track in high school because it was too boring, and switched to baseball.

One of his best sports was gymnastics. However, gymnastics is not a sport for large people. Robinson, who stood only five feet five inches when he was fourteen, began to grow. By his senior year he had sprouted all the way up to six feet six inches. That was too much body to whirl around in gymnastics.

Just before David's senior year, his father retired from the Navy. The family moved off base to Manassas, Virginia, just outside Washington, D.C. When David Robinson showed up for classes at Osbourne Park High School, the basketball team was excited. The players looked at this tall newcomer and hoped he could put that size to use on their team.

However, Robinson was not interested in trying basketball again. He sometimes played a game of basketball with friends, but he did not really enjoy it. According to Robinson, "The game didn't come naturally to me. I had no particular gift for it. I was just a tall kid." He was also well aware of how little he knew about the fine points of the game that most high school players had learned years before. In the end, however, Robinson finally gave in to the pressure and went out for the team.

Robinson displayed surprising coordination while playing for Osbourne Park. Still, he found basketball to be more work

The submarine piers at Norfolk, Virginia. Ambrose Robinson was stationed here.

than fun. He was placed near the basket to take advantage of his height, and there he was knocked around by stronger, more aggressive players. Robinson's coach could tell the kid's heart was not really into this kind of action. He worried that his center might lose all interest.

There were, in fact, many times when Robinson could hardly wait for the season to end. "I just wanted to stick it out so I could get my letter." Robinson did stick it out. In fact, he played so well that he was voted his team's most valuable player, and was named to the All-Metro second team. That was all very interesting and a little surprising to David. It did not mean much to him, however. Far more important to him was the spectacular score he achieved on his college entrance exam in his senior year. That cleared the way for Robinson to attend the United States Naval Academy in Annapolis, Maryland, in the fall of 1983.

Had Robinson started his growth spurt earlier, he would have been turned down by the Navy. Because of the limited space on Navy ships and airplanes, the Naval Academy does not accept very tall applicants. Most entrants must be six-feet six-inches or under, with a few exceptions made for persons up to six-feet eight-inches.

Ambrose Robinson, at six-feet six-inches, had barely slipped under the limit. David squeezed in by a hair's width. At the time he entered the academy he was bumping the six-feet eight-inch barrier. Fortunately for Robinson, once a person is accepted into the academy, he can remain even if he grows past the limit. Within weeks after entering the academy, Robinson shot past the upper height limit. To everyone's surprise, he was not nearly finished growing.

Chapter 3

Not every young adult can thrive under the discipline of a military academy. Life at the academy is strictly controlled by rules. Freedoms that many take for granted, such as keeping radios in the bedroom and running out for a bite of fast food late at night, are taken away.

Yet, Robinson enjoyed life at Navy. His logical, probing mind loved the structure and order of his schedule. He dove into the mental challenges of advanced calculus, computer science, and physics. Some of the more difficult Navy requirements helped him learn a few things about himself. Robinson despaired when he heard of the Navy drill that required him to swim for thirty minutes without stopping. Then he discovered, to his surprise, that he could do it. That led him to have more confidence in himself.

Navy also had a basketball team—as if that really mattered. Although still not especially fond of the game, Robinson agreed to build on the surprising success he had found at Osbourne Park.

Basketball had always been a low-key sport at Navy. The

David Robinson studies computer printout data at the United States Naval Academy.

Academy's height restrictions worked against it. Navy players were always shorter than their opponents, especially at the center position. Also Naval Academy graduates were required to serve full time in the Navy for five years after graduation. Any young players talented enough to consider playing pro ball would have been crazy to go to Navy. As a result Navy had not had an All-American in basketball since Elliott Loughlin back in 1933. The academy had not even qualified for the National Collegiate Athletic Association (NCAA) post-season tournament since 1966.

Navy Coach Paul Evans could hardly believe his good fortune when this graceful, six-feet nine-inch athlete walked onto the court. Robinson was already the tallest player in Navy history, and he was still growing. Yet he was coordinated enough to earn an A in gymnastics at the academy.

Evans's surprise turned to amazement when he discovered how little Robinson actually knew about basketball. Evans tried to look on the bright side of this inexperience. Robinson had picked up "no bad habits from the playground," according to Evans. "It's like teaching a ninth grader who wants to learn."

Before long, however, Evans began to doubt whether Robinson wanted to learn. The freshman just did not seem that interested in the game. As one assistant coach admitted, "He's not exactly a coach's player."

Robinson's progress was halted before he had a chance to show his coaches what he could do in his first year. During a boxing class, Robinson injured his hand so badly that he had to sit out the first four games of the season. When David finally got into a game, he barely touched the ball. Robinson's first game numbers read "0 points, 1 rebound."

Robinson did not break into the starting lineup all season. The basketball squad was one of the best to play at Navy in many years, and the team did not seem to need him. When he did play, Robinson struggled at the free-throw line. With only 195 pounds on his six-foot nine-inch frame, he took his lumps from older more muscular opponents. Still he improved steadily. He finished the 1983–84 season averaging 7.6 points, 4.0 rebounds, and 1.3 blocked shots per game as Navy accomplished its first 20-win season in history. Modest as those statistics seem, they were not bad for a beginning, and Robinson earned his conference's Rookie of the Year award.

This taste of big-time college competition aroused Robinson's interest in basketball. During the summer of 1984 he played against tough competition in the Washington Urban Coalition League. Robinson lifted weights with a vengeance, and added 20 pounds of muscle, mostly to his upper body. He also continued to grow. When he reported for practice in his sophomore season, he towered over his teammates at six-feet eleven-inches.

Robinson's new size and strength alone were enough to earn him the starting spot at center. He opened the season by outplaying some smaller opponents. While observers were impressed, they wondered what would happen when Robinson was matched up against a capable big man.

They found out in December 1984. Navy traveled to the Midwest to play in a tournament against Southern Illinois and Western Illinois, both of which had strong pivot players. The Navy sophomore dominated the tournament with 68 points and 31 rebounds. For basketball fans throughout the country who had never heard of Robinson, it was an eye-opening performance. It also opened Robinson's eyes. For the first time he began to realize how good he could be at this game.

If Coach Evans thought Robinson would now dedicate his life to the game, he was wrong. Evans once visited Robinson at his home to talk to him about basketball. According to the

Like many of Robinson's basketball coaches, Navy coach Paul Evans
was puzzled as to how to handle his reluctant star center.

coach, Robinson "spent the whole time showing me a television he had put together." During practice he worked hard, but continued to show little enthusiasm for the game. Teammates invited him to join them for extra workouts at the gym. Robinson couldn't believe they were serious. He had far too many things to do to bother spending any time practicing on his own. "Basketball is just something else to do," he told his dad.

Yet he finished the 1984–85 season with a 23.6 scoring average, 11.6 rebounds, and 4.0 blocks per game. Thanks to Robinson, Navy earned its first trip to the NCAA championships in more than a quarter century. In three short years, despite treating the game as merely something to fill his spare time, Robinson had become a college star. In fact, pro scouts who had never heard of Robinson a year before were now calling him one of the best big man prospects in the college ranks.

As Robinson began to realize how easily he could dominate a basketball game, he had to rethink his future. Suppose he really was good enough to be a pro star? Once a midshipman, as Navy undergraduates were called, entered his junior year at the academy, he was committed to five years of service after graduation. Some experts, such as Washington Bullets general manager Bob Ferry, thought that something could be worked out even if Robinson stayed in the Navy. "Robinson is so good, I'd take him on weekends," Ferry said.

However, most agreed that the five-year hitch would badly hurt, and probably ruin, any chance of a pro career. By staying at Navy, Robinson could be throwing away millions of dollars. Reluctantly, he had to consider abandoning ship at the Naval Academy.

"Basically, I was scared," Robinson said later. "Would I be comfortable anywhere else?" Navy was where he felt most at home, where he had always wanted to be. In the end, Robinson put loyalty to the Navy and to his other interests over a basketball career.

Robinson was praised for not letting the almighty dollar rule his life, for choosing to serve his country instead of his own self-interest. Even though he did make a sacrifice to stay, Robinson denied that he was quite the saint that many gave him credit for. He later said, "You can assume that if they had shown inflexibility or heartlessness, I would have walked the other way."

In fact, there had been a number of meetings between Robinson and Navy officials to work out a solution to his awkward situation. The Navy desperately wanted to keep Robinson. Not only did he give a good impression of the Navy with his basketball play, but he was a well-mannered, clean-cut, intelligent spokesman. David Robinson was a walking, slam-dunking advertisement for recruiting young people to join the Navy.

There were even better grounds for making exceptions in Robinson's case. His late growth spurt had pushed him to near seven feet. A man his size simply could not perform active duty on either a ship or an airplane. Through no fault of his own, Robinson's value to the Navy as anything other than a spokesman/role model was limited. In view of all this, Robinson and the Navy agreed to share the sacrifice. It was privately understood that Robinson's five-year active duty obligation would be reduced to two years.

Chapter 4

Now that Robinson had his sights on a NBA career, Coach Evans expected his junior center would have no trouble focusing his attention on the game. For Robinson, though, there was far more to life than just basketball. Evans's dream player turned into a coach's nightmare. The coach grew frustrated with his star's practice habits.

It was hard to believe that a player as good as Robinson was playing the game sheerly for enjoyment, and was not that concerned with wins and statistics. Evans tried to motivate him by screaming at him. During one practice, he threw Robinson out for lack of effort.

Such tactics may work with some players, but it was exactly the wrong thing to do with Robinson. For Robinson, problems were solved by analyzing the situation and discovering the solution. He was not used to being yelled at, and it only made him angry at his coach. Communication between Evans and Robinson worsened.

The friction hardly seemed necessary. Even if Robinson spent his time playing piano or building electronic equipment or working out mathematical brain teasers, he was still the best center in college basketball. He scored 33 points and grabbed 20 rebounds against George Mason College. Robinson swatted away 14 shot attempts against the University of North Carolina-Wilmington, a NCAA record. He scored 37 points against Delaware, and pulled down 25 rebounds in a game against Fairfield University.

For the 1985–86 season, the Navy center averaged 22.7 points and 13.0 rebounds per game. But the statistic that really caught the scouts' eyes was his 207 blocked shots (5.9 per game). That shattered the all-time college record. In fact, only one team—national champion Louisville—blocked as many shots as Robinson did by himself that year!

Not everyone was impressed by Robinson's numbers. After all, colleges such as Fairfield and George Mason were not considered to be college powerhouses. Navy played a fairly weak schedule, and not everyone was convinced that Robinson could handle tough competition.

The big test came when Navy was invited to the NCAA tournament again in the spring of 1986. After defeating Tulsa in its opening game, Navy was matched against powerful Syracuse. Syracuse's talented front line was far better than anything Robinson had faced before. Syracuse had also been battle-hardened from a season of play against rugged Big East Conference opponents.

Instead of backing away from Syracuse's bruising front line, Robinson went on the attack. Navy's guards kept feeding the ball inside to Robinson who took it straight to the basket. Although he was fouled repeatedly, Robinson kept banging away. He was awarded 27 foul shots and he sank 21 of them, both Navy records. Led by Robinson's effort, Navy pulled off a shocking 97-85 upset on Syracuse's home court.

Navy advanced against another giant killer, Cleveland

State. Although intimidated by nine Robinson blocks, the Vikings threatened to break open the game late in the second half. Robinson almost single-handedly answered each Cleveland State flurry. He scored 12 of Navy's final 16 points, including a shot with six seconds remaining that sealed the victory. The victory put underdog Navy into the final group of eight schools vying for the NCAA championship.

In the quarterfinals Navy was easily outgunned by a well-balanced Duke squad. Robinson, the man who had never taken the game seriously before, was stung by the defeat and embarrassed by his team's performance.

When the season was over, Robinson joined the United States 1986 World Championship team. By this time, he had earned so much respect that he was considered the key to the American title hopes. The Soviet Union was favored to win the competition because of its star center, Arvidas Sabonis. Robinson was the only American who had the size and talent to compare with the seven-foot two-inch Sabonis. If Robinson could at least slow down Sabonis, the Americans might have a chance.

Robinson played well as the United States advanced to the final round against the Soviet Union. Spurred by the challenge of playing against the best, he came alive in the finals. Robinson outplayed the Soviet star, especially in the crucial closing minutes, as the United States team won the championship.

Robinson returned for his senior season in a positive frame of mind. Coach Evans had left to take another job and was replaced by Pete Hermann. Hermann's milder approach to the game suited Robinson perfectly. "He allowed me to be myself, so I worked harder," Robinson said. While he kept up all his other interests, he was all business on the basketball court.

No one had to tell Robinson when he was not doing his

Robinson demonstrates the form that made him the most feared shot blocker in the college game.

job. The towering center was well aware of any subpar performance and was burning for a chance to redeem himself. During his senior year, Robinson followed up every poor showing with an outstanding game. After scoring only 8 points in a loss to the University of Richmond, Robinson broke loose for 45 points and 21 rebounds against James Madison University. He pounded inside for 43 points and 16 rebounds against a strong Michigan State team after scoring just 13 points against lightly regarded Utica College.

When Navy needed a clutch basket, Robinson was the man to take the shot. His ten-foot turnaround jump shot at the buzzer defeated Michigan State, 91-90. Another turnaround jumper, this time from 17 feet, pulled out a 67-66 win over UNC-Wilmington. With time running out against James Madison, Robinson was forced to throw up a desperation shot from about 40 feet. The ball banked off the glass and into the net for a 73-71 Navy victory!

Robinson increased his scoring average to 28.2, third best among NCAA players. He ranked fourth in rebounding at 11.8 per game. His reputation as a shot blocker scared away many opponents from driving into the lane. His blocked shot total went down as a result, but he still led the nation in that category with 144 (4.5 per game). Robinson was voted the College Player of the Year by nearly every organization making such an award.

Robinson saved his best performance for the toughest teams. On January 25, 1987, Navy traveled to Kentucky to take on the highly ranked Wildcats. There were no mental lapses that day; Robinson owned the air above the basket. On defense he stuffed 10 shots back in the faces of Kentucky shooters, and snatched 14 rebounds. On offense he scored 45 of his team's 69 points. Robinson made 17 of 22 shots and sank 11 of 12 free throws for 45 points. Navy lost the game by

The San Antonio Spurs selected David Robinson with the first pick in the 1987 NBA draft. However, it would be two years before he would play his first professional game.

a score of 80-69, but the team's center gained new respect that day.

Robinson finished his career in style. Navy drew the fast-breaking University of Michigan in its first-round contest of the 1987 NCAA tournament. Robinson played his heart out. He hit on 22 of 37 shots from the field and totaled 50 points, setting a new Navy record. Yet it was not enough as the Wolverines raced to a 97-82 win.

Pro scouts who watched David Robinson soar over the court against Kentucky and Michigan rated him as the best pro prospect of the 1987 draft. Since he was still learning the game, there was a good chance that he could continue to improve. Unfortunately, the team that drafted him would have to wait before Robinson could play for them. The big center owed two years of active duty to the Navy before he could play pro ball.

The woeful San Antonio Spurs had first choice in the 1987 draft. The team was so dreadful that it was losing fans and money. As badly as they needed quick improvement, the Spurs decided that Robinson was worth the wait. They made him the first selection of the draft.

Chapter 5

Robinson graduated from the Naval Academy in 1987 with a degree in mathematics. His first assignment as an officer was to help supervise construction at the Navy's Trident submarine base at Kings Bay in southeastern Georgia.

Robinson quickly realized how sheltered he had been all his life, first at home and then at the Naval Academy. "I was scared to death," he said of his first experience out on his own. Robinson's eyes were opened to serious issues such as race relations. The fact that he was black had not been a major issue in his life, even though he was aware of being the only black student in many classes. He remembered few unpleasant incidents.

In Georgia, though, Robinson saw the gap that separated black and white. The sight of people struggling to survive in run-down shelters haunted him, especially in view of the huge salary the Spurs would pay him. "It's hard to be a good person if you're rich," Robinson said. "My biggest fear is that I won't be a good person."

Few people who met the classy, respectful Robinson were

concerned about that. A number of basketball experts, however, worried about Robinson's basketball future. Robinson became so involved in his Navy assignment that he left little time for basketball. The first sign that the big center had lost something on his game came in the 1987 Pan-American Games. Robinson averaged only 14 points a game for a United States team that failed to win the gold medal.

Then, in March 1988, an Army squad thumped Robinson's Navy team, 118-71 in a tournament. Robinson was in such poor shape that one observer reported he could not get down the court three times in a row. The rust continued to show when a team of United States Olympic hopefuls went on a tour of Europe. Robinson provided little offense. One of his teammates complained, "He doesn't act like he's into these games at all."

Robinson's slump continued into the Olympics, where he clashed with coach John Thompson. Thompson was an intimidating leader, nearly as tall as Robinson and much larger. He expected his players to follow instructions without question, which was not Robinson's nature.

"Thompson wanted me to run into a brick wall," said Robinson. "I analyze things."

The tension took its toll as the team stumbled badly. The United States could not make a serious run at the Soviet Union in its contest. Despite the presence of stars such as Kansas All-American Danny Manning, the team settled for third place. That was the worst finish ever for a United States team in the Olympics. Much of the blame went to Robinson for his lackluster 12.8 points and 6.8 rebounds per game. Suddenly the Spurs' investment did not seem like such a good deal.

When Robinson reported to San Antonio, coach Larry Brown saw immediately that the two-year layoff had hurt him.

Yet he also saw flashes of incredible raw talent. On July 25, 1989, Brown turned his new center loose in an intra-squad game against other rookies and free agents. Robinson looked more like the Navy terror of old than the Olympic disappointment. He was a one-man magnetic force field around the basket as he blocked 14 shots.

During the pre season Robinson learned the hard way why pros laugh when they hear basketball described as a non-contact sport. The bumping, shoving, and elbowing for position was fierce. "I expected physical play," Robinson said. "But not this bad." Although he had built up bulging biceps through lifting weights, Robinson found that he could not overpower pro centers. Most outweighed him by about twenty pounds. Nor did he have many one-on-one offensive moves. He saw that he would have to rely on his speed and athletic ability to be successful.

"Run, run, run!" Robinson thought to himself while on the court. He knew that no one his size could stay with him in a sprint. He could outrun his heavier opponents to the basket for easy dunks.

Lieutenant Robinson was pleased to be playing for San Antonio. A shy loner much of his life, he was pleased to find that teammate Terry Cummings shared his interest in music. The two spent time together, playing and singing songs that they composed. Robinson also felt at ease in San Antonio. He preferred it to the pressure of a huge place such as New York.

His first NBA game brought exactly the kind of headline matchup he wanted to avoid. Magic Johnson and the flashy Los Angeles Lakers were coming to town. Robinson ignored the media attention and stood up to the punishment the Lakers dished out. In the first quarter he drew three fouls while battling for position.

During the third period the Spurs clung to a slim lead.

A noncontact sport? Robinson bangs bodies on a drive to the hoop.

Magic Johnson drove into the lane for the tying basket. Robinson ignored the veteran's fakes and stayed with him. As Johnson layed the ball up to the basket, Robinson flicked it away. That was as close as the Lakers would get. With Robinson scoring 23 points and taking 17 rebounds, the Spurs won, 106-98.

After the game Johnson had news for Robinson-doubters. "Some rookies are never really rookies," he noted. "Robinson is one of them."

Over in the Spurs' locker room Robinson unintentionally demonstrated his wide range of abilities. Asked about his block against Magic Johnson, he responded, "My job is to keep the opponent from taking the ball to the hoop with impunity." None of the reporters could remember hearing a player describe a play in quite that way before. Then again, none of them had interviewed a pro center who had read the dictionary as a child!

Although Robinson soaked up lessons from his coach and teammates in practice, he did not always enjoy the success of his first season. Sometimes he would tune out his surroundings and wander around the court in a fog. Some critics thought Robinson's wide range of interests blocked his path to greatness. The rookie brushed off the criticism. "Funny," he said, "most of the time they want athletes to take a little more interest in the rest of life."

There were certain players on whom Robinson had no trouble focusing. Ever since he had reported to camp, experts had compared him to the reigning "towers of power" in the NBA, Hakeem Olajuwon of Houston and Patrick Ewing of New York. Olajuwon was a Nigerian who, like Robinson, did not begin playing basketball until well into his teens. Quickness, strength, and athletic skill had made Olajuwon the NBA's top center. Olajuwon was the defending NBA

Setting picks is a thankless but important part of a center's job. Here Robinson lays one on all-star guard John Stockton.

rebounding champion and had finished tenth in scoring the previous year.

The stronger, more ferocious Ewing was Olajuwon's main competition for the top spot. Ewing, a Jamaican who moved to the United States at the age of eleven, had recently perfected a deadly selection of offensive moves to go with his already tough defense.

If Robinson wanted to be the best, these were the men he would have to pass. Both Olajuwon and Ewing had heard about Robinson and were determined to prove they were still the kings of the hill. Fans eagerly awaited Robinson's first clash against these giants. Two months into the season, Olajuwon and the Houston Rockets came to San Antonio. The two big men battled furiously, constantly forcing the other away from his favorite shots. Robinson more than held his own. Although Olajuwon won the rebounding battle, Robinson outscored him, 19 to 15. The Spurs' center badgered his more experienced rival into missing 12 of his 17 shots.

A month later Robinson took on Ewing and the Knicks in New York. Ewing was as eager to defend his turf as the new challenger was to take it. The two lanky centers locked so tightly in the key that they looked like a giant octopus. Ewing forced Robinson into six turnovers. Still, David stood his ground against the heavier Ewing and even blocked two of his shots.

Late in the game Ewing staked out a position near the free-throw line. He backed into Robinson so hard that Robinson stumbled ten feet backward. New York's Gerald Wilkins saw Ewing standing alone and fired a pass to him. Robinson recovered very quickly, intercepting the pass and starting a fast break. New York won the game, 107-101, but again Robinson outscored his rival. He ended up with 27 points to Ewing's 18.

Robinson has been a fixture on the NBA All-Defensive team since entering the league.

Although he had plenty of help from teammates such as Terry Cummings, Maurice Cheeks, and Sean Elliott, Robinson deserved most of the credit for leading San Antonio to the most dramatic about-face in NBA history. The Spurs, who had finished 21-61 the previous year, came alive to post a 56-26 mark in 1989–90. Robinson finished second in the NBA in rebounding with a 12.0 average, third in blocked shots (3.8 average), and tenth in scoring (24.3). That performance earned him every vote in the balloting for Rookie of the Year.

The Spurs roared through the first round of the playoffs, sweeping the Denver Nuggets in three games. Robinson stepped up his effort to average more than 28 points and 13 rebounds in the series. The ease of their win left the Spurs unprepared for a more typical playoff series against Portland. The Trail Blazers danced on the Spurs in Game 1. Robinson, playing in a fog, made only 3 of 11 shots.

The embarrassing effort woke him up. Robinson dominated the front line play as San Antonio recovered to win two of the next three games. Then Portland finished off the Spurs in two close games. Robinson's first year as a pro was over. Fans wondered if Robinson would be different now that he knew how good he could be. Would he get hooked on basketball and back away from his other interests?

Not a chance. When Robinson reported to training camp in the fall of 1990, he was carrying a new toy. He had become fascinated with the music of the saxophone and was determined to teach himself to play.

Chapter 6

The young Spurs shot off to a fast start in the 1990–91 season. With a year's experience behind him, Robinson felt more comfortable taking the court against the NBA giants. He scored more, rebounded more, and blocked more shots than in his first season.

Everything seemed to be going his way. People admired his manners; his open, honest communication; and the way he honored his commitment to the Navy. He treated fans well and they adored him. Once he stopped to pump gasoline at a self-service station in San Antonio. He was soon mobbed by fans who recognized him. Robinson patiently stood in the rain signing autographs for all the fans.

Robinson's glowing reputation was enhanced by a shoe company. They brought out a series of popular "Mr. Robinson's Neighborhood" ads. Robinson's popularity grew so quickly that he received more All-Star votes from fans than any other Western Conference player in the 1990–91 balloting.

Robinson enjoyed living in San Antonio. Now that he was

a wealthy celebrity, the shy Robinson suddenly had no trouble finding dates. Still, he was not a party person. "Learning stuff" was what he most enjoyed doing, and he preferred quiet activities at home. He liked living close to his parents, for whom he bought a house in San Antonio.

A season that started out so promising, however, soon began to go sour. The Spurs were hobbled by a series of injuries to key players. With those players out of the lineup, Robinson had to step up and provide more scoring punch. That was when the flaws in Robinson's game began to show. As he later admitted, "I came into this league with almost no offense." Almost all his points came on fast breaks, rebounds, dunks, or free throws. When the Spurs passed the ball to Robinson in the low post, he did not know what to do with it. Although he owned a soft, left-handed jump shot, he had trouble getting into position to use it.

As Robinson and the Spurs struggled, Coach Brown commented, "When I see Ewing or Olajuwon play, David isn't there yet."

Meanwhile, events halfway around the globe brought Robinson face to face with the grim side of life. On January 16, 1991, Robinson was dressing for a game with the Dallas Mavericks when word came of war with Iraq in the Persian Gulf. Upon hearing reports of the first bombing runs, "my stomach just dropped," Robinson said. Many of his Navy friends were sailing the warships and flying bombing missions. Were it not for his fluke growth spurt, Robinson would probably have been among them.

Robinson sat glued to the television set in the locker room until game time. San Antonio won the contest by a score of 100-94, but Robinson's heart was not in it. "The war makes the significance of this game very small. I've only been in mock situations and those were not fun at all. They

Once timid on offense, Robinson now searches out an opponent's weakness and attacks.

give you a real sense of the reality of war. It's a sobering experience."

The turmoil of the war affected Robinson's play. He insisted that he blocked it out of his mind while on the court, but he lacked his usual aggressiveness. The Spurs wasted a number of huge leads during that period, winning only 10 of 19 games.

By the time the fighting ended in March, the Spurs had fallen back into a wild scramble for the division lead. The Utah Jazz and the Houston Rockets both caught the stumbling Spurs late in the season. It was time for Robinson to prove that the space around the basket really was "Mr. Robinson's Neighborhood."

In the last weeks of the season, Robinson stalked opposing players with the quickness and cunning he had shown earlier. Those careless enough to challenge Robinson could suffer their choice of humiliations. Robinson could either strip the ball from them before they got their shot off, or leap high to block the shot if they did get it off. On two occasions he swatted away 11 shots in a single game.

There was no way for a team to play a normal game with Robinson terrorizing the court. In the words of Matt Goukas, coach of the Charlotte Hornets, "He distorts your whole game." Robinson distorted enough games so that the Spurs were able to edge out Houston in the season's final game to win the Midwest crown.

Robinson improved in every area of his game during his second season. With Olajuwon injured for part of the year, Robinson easily won the NBA rebounding title with an average of 13 per game. He boosted his scoring average to 25.6, to rank ninth. He also led the league in blocked shots.

Robinson leaped past Ewing and Olajuwon to win the sportswriters' vote as the NBA's top center in 1991. In a

Robinson fights for inside position against Utah Jazz muscleman Karl Malone, one of the league's premier power forwards.

computerized rating of basketball players published by *The Sporting News* in 1991, Robinson ranked with Michael Jordan as the two top players in the NBA. After hearing so much talk about Robinson's lack of experience, New Jersey Nets guard Mookie Blaylock could only mutter, "If he's still learning the game, I'd hate to see him when he knows it stone cold."

Robinson was the main reason that San Antonio entered the 1991 playoffs as one of the favorites to win the NBA championship. The Spurs' first round opponent, Golden State, appeared to be an easy victim. The Warriors had the second worst record among Western Conference playoff teams. They had no center who could challenge Robinson.

Golden State did not even try to match up against the Spurs' center. Instead, they used a coaching gimmick. They went with a small, quick lineup, often using four guards on the court at one time. Robinson played well as the teams split the first two games of the series, averaging 28 points and 13 rebounds. After awhile, however, he began to look like a man trying to catch squirrels. The smaller Golden State team shocked the Spurs by taking the series three games to one.

Robinson was deeply disappointed by the early exit from the playoffs. "This is tough," he said to reporters afterward. "I don't feel like I fulfilled my responsibilities."

At the end of the 1990–91 season Robinson was a confused man. Publicly he stated, "I wouldn't trade places with anyone. I'm having the best time in the world."

Yet he wasn't having the best time in the world. Robinson took a look at his life and the way he was living it and didn't like what he saw. He felt as though he had spent his whole life learning and growing and trying to become a better person. Now, during his two pro seasons, he was going backward. Although he was still polite and widely respected, he detected that the fame and fortune were going to his head. He was becoming selfish and getting into bad habits such as being late for practice. If he continued to slide, what would become of him when his glory years in the NBA were over?

"What surprised me was that I wasn't happy," Robinson remembers. "Here I had everything I wanted. I looked at myself and I didn't like the person I was becoming."

Although he had gone to church to please his mother, Robinson had never been particularly religious. He paid little attention to the Spurs' team chaplain. When locker room evangelist Greg Ball asked to talk with him, Robinson repeatedly found excuses to avoid him.

Finally, though, Robinson agreed to give Ball a few minutes to say what he had to say. To Robinson's astonishment, Ball seemed to know exactly what was bothering him. Robinson had no purpose to his life. He just kind of wandered around, dabbling at whatever interested him at the time. He had no commitment to anything. Ball urged Robinson to turn to the Bible to provide a focus for his life.

The few minutes ended up being a five-hour conversation. A week later, June 8, 1991, Robinson received a private baptism and committed himself to a new Christian life.

One of the first things he did with his newly found purpose was to call up Valerie Hoggat. He had met Valerie while on Naval duty in Port Hueneme, California, back in 1988. The two had then dated frequently for a time even after Robinson returned to Georgia. Robinson had suddenly cut off the relationship. Now Robinson was ashamed at how selfishly he had acted toward Valerie. The two got back together and began reading the Bible together.

Three months later David asked Valerie to marry him. The proposal took Valerie by surprise. Training camp for the next season was about to start. There wouldn't even be time for a

Although the Spurs depend on him to score, Robinson knows when to pass off to an open teammate.

honeymoon. Robinson said he now knew what he wanted and didn't want. Valerie accepted.

So the newly married Robinson entered the preseason in a completely different frame of mind than the past. Although he still enjoyed his music, electronics, and other interests, he was focusing on basketball. He now saw his talent as coming from God, and his career was a chance to give glory to God.

Robinson came to the court armed with a new battle cry. "Don't you know you're standing against the armies of the Lord?" he challenged opponents. "I'm out here to honor God, and if you're not here to do that, then you're going down today."

Starting with this season, Robinson was dedicating himself to becoming the best basketball player he could be. Robinson's new focus did not show immediate results on the court. In his third season, 1991–92, his statistics actually took a slight dip. Robinson averaged 23.2 points and 12.2 rebounds per game. Furthermore, he and his teammates again failed to get past the early rounds of the playoffs.

The highlight of his year came after the NBA season. Robinson was selected to play on the 1992 United States Olympic basketball team. The team was so loaded with NBA stars such as Michael Jordan, Larry Bird, Magic Johnson, Charles Barkley, and Patrick Ewing that the media named it the "Dream Team."

Some critics argued against the United States sending their best pro players to the Olympics. No other Olympic team could hope to compete against this All-Star lineup. However, Robinson had been burned before when the United States used only college players on its Olympic team. It was payback time. "I went to the Naval Academy," he told reporters, "and I say if you're going to war, send your best troops and support them."

Robinson alternated with his NBA rival Ewing at center for the Dream Team. He and his teammates romped through the Olympics. They won their games by an average of nearly 44 points. After the team overwhelmed Croatia, 117-85, in the championship game, Robinson finally had settled an old score—he had won his gold medal.

Chapter 7

Robinson put up another solid season in 1992–93. His 23.4 points and 11.7 rebounds per game were nearly identical to his previous year's totals. This time, though, Robinson seemed primed for the big games. He dominated the inside play during the NBA All-Star game, with 21 points and 10 rebounds in limited playing time. He led the way as the Spurs jumped out to a two-games-to-one lead in their opening playoff series against Portland.

The Trail Blazers fought back in Game 4. With less than a minute to play, Portland captured the lead. With the game on the line, Robinson called for the ball. He slipped through Portland's defense to bank home a layup, winning the game and the best-of-five series.

The Spurs then played hard against the favored Phoenix Suns. Phoenix led the best-of-seven series, three games to two, going into Game 6 at San Antonio. The teams battled furiously. With the score tied at 100-100 and the clock ticking down, the game appeared headed for overtime. Then Charles Barkley launched an arching shot just over Robinson's outstretched fingers just before time ran out. The ball went through the net, and the Spurs again headed home in defeat.

"It was a tough way to lose," said Robinson. "Especially at home."

By this time, a new rival was storming onto the NBA scene to challenge Robinson. Shaquille O'Neal, who was as tall as Robinson but a good sixty pounds heavier, was beginning to throw his weight around for the Orlando Magic. The colorful Shaq attracted attention wherever he went.

Robinson and some other veteran NBA centers were irritated by the fuss over O'Neal. Although the Magic center had awesome potential, he had not yet accomplished anything in the pros. Furthermore, O'Neal played a rough power game with lots of banging bodies. This sometimes caused tempers to flare. Hard feelings led to a more bitter rivalry than anything Robinson had experienced with Ewing and Olajuwon.

Robinson, normally respectful of everyone, bristled when the subject of O'Neal came up. "He talks about people being jealous of him but he has nothing I want," said Robinson.

The rivalry flared white hot when both Robinson and O'Neal went on scoring sprees in 1993–94. By this time Robinson had added several new weapons to his offense. He used his quickness to drive around defenders, especially from the left side. He developed an accurate left-handed jump shot that nobody could block. By mid-season the man who once admitted to having no offensive moves could say, "Nobody is really tough to score on."

With Michael Jordan retired, the NBA scoring crown was up for grabs for the first time in several years. Both Robinson and O'Neal took aim at it. Going into the final game of the season, O'Neal led Robinson by the slightest of margins. Both were averaging about 29 points per game.

The Spurs thought that Robinson deserved the scoring

A natural left-hander, Robinson drives most effectively from the left side of the court.

title. They told him that they planned to set up their teammate for shots whenever possible against the Los Angeles Clippers. Robinson accepted the challenge. He started strong in the first period. He hit shots from close range, medium range, and from the foul line.

Robinson scored 18 points before any of his teammates made a basket. Seeing what the Spurs were up to, the Clippers concentrated on stopping Robinson. They managed to slow him down. Yet at the end of three quarters, Robinson had 43 points. That might have been enough but Robinson and the Spurs weren't taking any chances. In the final period Robinson went wild. He put on a dazzling display of dunks and jump shots. He even connected on a long three-point shot, something he rarely attempted.

Robinson left the court giddy with exhaustion. "It was fun," he told reporters. "I really had a good time." When the calculators totaled up the damage Robinson had inflicted on the Clippers, Robinson ended up with a career-high 71 points! Even more impressive was his accuracy. He made 26 of his 41 shots from the field and 18 of 25 free throws.

The performance impressed everyone but Shaquille O'Neal. O'Neal's 32 points in his last game left him with a 29.3 scoring average. With 71 points, Robinson jumped past O'Neal to claim the scoring championship with a 29.8 average. O'Neal thought Robinson's title was undeserved. "I heard that no defense was played," he complained.

However, Los Angeles Clippers Coach Bob Weiss insisted that Robinson had earned his title. "Robinson was spectacular," said Weiss. "We double-teamed him with our forwards every time but he still scored the points."

The Spurs approached the playoffs believing they had found the missing ingredient for the title. Wild and unpredictable forward Dennis Rodman brought a toughness to the team that Robinson and the Spurs had lacked. Although Rodman's strange behavior, which included brightly dyed hair and a habit of breaking team rules, could be unsettling, he seemed eager to help the Spurs to the championship. "David's got so much talent it's ridiculous," said Rodman. "It's a pleasure to go out on the court with him."

Unfortunately, Rodman lost control in the Spurs' second game against the Utah Jazz. He committed a flagrant foul and a technical foul and got himself suspended for one game. Meanwhile, Robinson lapsed into a fog. He shot poorly against Utah and was unable to make up for Rodman's absence. The Spurs again fell out of the playoffs early.

Again failure only made Robinson more determined. He lifted weights in the off-season to build himself up to 245 pounds to help him battle the NBA giants.

During the 1994–95 season, Robinson could not care less whether O'Neal won the individual scoring title. He wanted only the team championship. He cut back a little on his scoring to blend in better with his teammates. Yet his 27.6 average placed him third in the league. He played such ferocious defense that he was an overwhelming choice as the NBA's top defensive center. Robinson ranked fourth in blocked shots, seventh in rebounding, and fifteenth in steals. No other player contributed as much to his team.

The NBA rewarded Robinson's effort by voting him the league's Most Valuable Player for the season. With Robinson leading the way, the Spurs played remarkably consistent basketball. They never lost more than two games in a row as they roared to a 62-20 mark—the NBA's best.

However, could the Spurs come through in the playoffs? In the opening round, the Spurs bounced the Denver Nuggets in three straight games. They thrashed the Los Angeles Lakers in the first two games of their best-of-seven series. At last the Spurs seemed to be rolling toward a title.

Robinson talks over strategy with point guard Avery Johnson, whose main job is to get the ball to Robinson.

Then turmoil struck again. During Game 3 in Los Angeles, Dennis Rodman refused to take part in team huddles. The Spurs lost the game. San Antonio Coach Bob Hill then suspended Rodman for Game 4.

Robinson responded by taking over Rodman's rebounding role in addition to his other duties. In game four Robinson scored 26 points, grabbed 22 rebounds, and stifled the Lakers with his defense. The Spurs won, 80-71. Robinson then finished off the Lakers in game six. He snuffed out a Lakers rally by scoring 12 of his team's final 14 points in a 100-88 win.

At last Robinson had earned a trip to the Western Conference Finals. There he faced an old rival, Hakeem Olajuwon. "This is definitely the biggest stakes that we've had since we started playing each other," said Robinson. He looked forward to the match. He had controlled Olajuwon easily this year as San Antonio beat the Houston Rockets in five of their six games.

Robinson started horribly in game one. He made only 1 of his first 11 shots. Although he rallied to finish with 21 points, Houston squeaked out a 94-93 win. Robinson responded with his best game of the series in game two. He torched Olajuwon for 32 points, including 14 in the final 12 minutes. However, Olajuwon was on a playoff roll that had started in the early rounds. Showing moves that no one had ever seen from a big man, he maneuvered around Robinson for 41 points. Houston won again.

Stunned, the Spurs held a team meeting. "Whatever misunderstandings we had everyone talked them out and now we're ready to go," Robinson declared. He was right. Although Olajuwon continued to shine, the Spurs won the next two games.

Again, distractions struck at the worst possible time. After showing up late for practice, Rodman was benched at the start of Game 5. The Spurs floundered. Olajuwon scored 42 points in Game 5 and 39 in Game 6 as the Rockets took the series.

After the success he had enjoyed that season, Robinson took the loss hard. "It felt like falling off a cliff," he said. "To go from something so high to something so low in such a short time. . . ." He felt especially bad because observers blamed him personally for the loss. Olajuwon had grossly outplayed him. Many thought this proved that Robinson had not deserved the MVP award.

Olajuwon came to Robinson's defense. Robinson was the reason why Olajuwon had played so brilliantly. "The baskets I get against David are not easy baskets," he explained. "He makes me work for them. That's why I respect him. He forces you to raise your game." Other observers noted that the Spurs asked Robinson to defend Olajuwon one-on-one, while the Rockets gave Olajuwon double-team help against Robinson. Yet none of this erased the pain of the defeat.

"All you can do is dig back in and get it going again." said Robinson. He went back to work in 1995–96, with familiar results. He led his team to a 59-23 record. He placed fifth in scoring, second in blocked shots, and pulled down more rebounds than anyone else in the league.

Unfortunately, the 1996 playoffs rang their same familiar note. Utah bounced the Spurs out of action in the second round. Again Robinson took the heat for the post-season failure.

Robinson redeemed himself somewhat with his performance on the 1996 United States Olympic team. His 28 points paced the latest Dream Team in its 95-69 gold medal victory over Yugoslavia.

The 1996–97 season was not nearly as satisfying. Due to injuries to his back and foot, Robinson appeared in just 6

Robinson defends the lane for the 1996 U.S. Olympic team. Robinson outshined teammates Shaquille O'Neal and Hakeem Olajuwon at center for the gold medal winners.

games. Without their star player the Spurs struggled to a last place finish. He will return healthy for the start of 1997–98.

Robinson's roller-coaster ride of success and disappointment never seems to end. Through it all, though, he has remained one of the NBA's solid citizens. San Antonio coach Bob Hill believes that his star's character is far more important than his skill. "I tell him 'David, you're the role model this league needs. You should be everywhere.'"

In fact, Robinson does his part to help the community. For example, in an effort to encourage children to focus on education, he promised a $2,000 college scholarship to every fifth grade student at a San Antonio elementary school who attended college. He prefers to spend most of his spare time at home attending to his family. In fact, he was so involved with his sons, David, Jr., and Corey, that he listed *The Little Mermaid* as his favorite movie on a team questionnaire.

Robinson's clean living habits and perfect posture sometimes make him look out of place among the rugged pro athletes. Yet no one questions his marvelous talent. Maybe that talent will one day take him to the top of the roller-coaster ride—the NBA title. If that happens Robinson will have surprised the critics who say he isn't tough enough or mean enough to win it all. However, it won't surprise a man who knows a thing or two about winning basketball games, Michael Jordan. "You look at Robinson," Jordan once commented, "and what is there that he can't do?"

Career Statistics

College

Year	Team	GP	FG%	REB	PTS	AVG
1983–84	U.S. Naval Academy	28	.623	111	214	7.6
1984–85	U.S. Naval Academy	32	.644	370	756	23.6
1985–86	U.S. Naval Academy	35	.607	455	796	22.7
1986–87	U.S. Naval Academy	32	.591	378	903	28.2
Totals		127	.613	1,314	2,669	21.0

NBA

Year	Team	GP	FG%	REB	AST	STL	BLK	PTS	AVG
1989–90	San Antonio	82	.531	983	164	138	319	1,993	24.3
1990–91	San Antonio	82	.552	1,063	208	127	320	2,101	25.6
1991–92	San Antonio	68	.551	829	181	158	305	1,578	23.2
1992–93	San Antonio	82	.501	956	301	127	264	1,916	23.4
1993–94	San Antonio	80	.507	855	381	139	265	2,383	29.8
1994–95	San Antonio	81	.530	877	236	134	262	2,238	27.6
1995–96	San Antonio	82	.516	1,000	247	111	271	2,051	25.0
1996–97	San Antonio	6	.500	51	8	6	6	106	17.7
Totals		563	.525	6,614	1,726	940	2,012	14,366	25.5

Where to Write David Robinson

Mr. David Robinson
c/o San Antonio Spurs
Alamodome
100 Montana Street
San Antonio, TX 78203

Index

Osbourne Park High School, 17, 19

P

Pan-American Games, 34
Persian Gulf War, 43, 44
Phoenix Suns, 51
Port Hueneme, California, 48
Portland Trail Blazers, 41, 51

R

Richmond, University of, 30
Robinson, Ambrose, 14–18
Robinson, Chuck, 16
Robinson, Corey, 60
Robinson, David
    All-Star, 42
    at Naval Academy, 19–25,
      26–32
    childhood, 14–16
    college player of the year, 30
    hobbies, 11, 15, 24, 26, 41
    in navy, 33–34
    intelligence, 11, 15, 18, 26–27
    "Mr. Robinson's Neighborhood,"
      42
    Most Valuable Player, 7, 55
    NBA Scoring Title, 52, 54
    Persian Gulf War, 43, 44
    personal crisis, 47, 48
    playoffs, 7, 9, 41, 47, 51–52, 55,
      57–58
    religious beliefs, 48–49
    San Antonio Spurs, joins, 34
    shot blocking, 27
    sports as a child, 16–18
    U.S. Olympic team, 34, 50, 58
Robinson, David, Jr., 60
Robinson, Freda, 14, 15, 17
Robinson, Kim, 16

Robinson, Valerie Hoggat, 48–49
Rodman, Dennis, 54–55, 57–58
Russell, Bill, 11

S

Sabonis, Arvidas, 28
Southern Illinois University, 22
Soviet Union, 28, 34
Sporting News, The, 47
Syracuse University, 27

T

Thompson, John, 34
Tulsa University, 27

U

United States Naval Academy, 11,
    18, 19–25, 26–30, 32
United States Navy, 14, 16, 17, 25
United States Olympic team, 34, 50,
    58
United States World Championship
    team, 1986, 28
Utah Jazz, 45, 55
Utica College, 30

V

Virginia Beach, Virginia, 15

W

Washington, D.C., 17
Washington Bullets, 24
Washington Urban Coalition League,
    22
Weiss, Bob, 54
Western Illinois University, 22
Wilkins, Gerald, 39

Y

Yugoslavia, 58